SLEEP TIGHT, SNOW WHITE

15 BEWITCHING BEDTIME RHYMES

JEN ARENA *illustrated by* **LORENA ALVAREZ**

ALFRED A. KNOPF  NEW YORK

Sleep tight,
Snow White.
Seven dwarves
say good night.

Rest your head,
Little Red.
Forget the Wolf.
It's time for bed.

Listen to me,
Princess and Pea.
If there's a lump,
just let it be.

Look at the clocks,
Goldilocks!
Brush your teeth.
Take off your socks.

Go to sleep,
Little Bo Peep.
Close your eyes and
count your sheep.

Want a fella,
Cinderella?
Eight hours' sleep
will make you *bella*.

Don't rough it,
Little Miss Muffet.
Fluff a pillow—
chuck the tuffet!

You're disarming,
dear Prince Charming,
but snore so loudly,
it's alarming!

Don't be mean,
Wicked Queen.
Start a new day,
fresh and clean.

Sleep's your duty,
Sleeping Beauty.
When you snooze,
you're such a cutie.

Day will fade,
Little Mermaid.
Rest underwater
in ocean shade.

Please settle,
Hansel and Gretel.
Sleepytime tea
is in the kettle.

Lie down at least,
Beauty and Beast.
Wait for sunrise
far to the east.

Time to chill,
Jack and Jill.
Dream of pails,
another hill.

Sad but true,
Little Boy Blue.
They're all asleep.
You should be, too!

For Clara —J.A.

To Elena and Florencio —L.A.

THIS IS A BORZOI BOOK PUBLISHED BY ALFRED A. KNOPF

Text copyright © 2017 by Jennifer Arena

Jacket art and interior illustrations copyright © 2017 by Lorena Alvarez

All rights reserved. Published in the United States by Alfred A. Knopf,

an imprint of Random House Children's Books, a division of Penguin Random House LLC, New York.

Knopf, Borzoi Books, and the colophon are registered trademarks of Penguin Random House LLC.

Visit us on the Web! randomhousekids.com

Educators and librarians, for a variety of teaching tools, visit us at RHTeachersLibrarians.com

Library of Congress Cataloging-in-Publication Data

Names: Arena, Jen, author. | Alvarez, Lorena, illustrator.

Title: Sleep tight, Snow White : bedtime rhymes / by Jen Arena ; illustrated by Lorena Alvarez.

Description: First edition. | New York : Alfred A. Knopf, [2017] | Summary: Bedtime rhymes

for nursery rhyme and fairy tale characters.

Identifiers: LCCN 2016000216 | ISBN 978-1-101-93713-6 (trade) |

ISBN 978-1-101-93714-3 (lib. bdg.) | ISBN 978-1-101-93715-0 (ebook)

Subjects: | CYAC: Stories in rhyme. | Bedtime—Fiction. | Characters in literature—Fiction.

Classification: LCC PZ8.3.A58632 Sl 2017 | DDC [E]—dc23

The text of this book is set in 20-point Corona Medium.

The illustrations were created digitally.

MANUFACTURED IN CHINA

October 2017

2 4 6 8 10 9 7 5 3 1

First Edition